To my former neighbors, forever friends, and talented
critique buddies, Jill and Vivian.
Love, Maryann

To the lovely town of Montclair, New Jersey, whose unique,
free-thinking culture makes everyone feel like they belong.
—K. A. L.

Henry Holt and Company, *Publishers since 1866*
Henry Holt® is a registered trademark of Macmillan Publishing Group, LLC
120 Broadway, New York, NY 10271 • mackids.com

Library of Congress Cataloging-in-Publication Data
Names: Cocca-Leffler, Maryann, 1958–author. | Lombardi, Kristine A., illustrator.
Title: The belonging tree / Maryann Cocca-Leffler ; illustrated by Kristine A. Lombardi.
Description: First edition. | New York : Henry Holt and Company, 2020. | "Christy Ottaviano Books." | Audience: Ages 3–7. | Audience: Grades K–1. |
Summary: A young squirrel disagrees with his parents who want to exclude such newcomers as the
blue jays, chipmunks, and beavers from their woodland neighborhood.
Identifiers: LCCN 2019038487 | ISBN 9781250305138 (hardcover)
Subjects: CYAC: Toleration—Fiction. | Prejudices—Fiction. | Squirrels—Fiction. | Forest animals—Fiction.
Classification: LCC PZ7.C638 Be 2020 | DDC [E]—dc23
LC record available at https://lccn.loc.gov/2019038487

Our books may be purchased in bulk for promotional, educational, or business use. Please contact your local bookseller or the
Macmillan Corporate and Premium Sales Department at (800) 221-7945 ext. 5442 or by email at MacmillanSpecialMarkets@macmillan.com.

First edition, 2020 | Design by Patrick Collins and Vera Soki
The artist used watercolor and Adobe Photoshop to create the illustrations for this book.
Printed in China by Toppan Leefung Printing Ltd., Dongguan City, Guangdong Province

1 3 5 7 9 10 8 6 4 2

THE Belonging Tree

MARYANN COCCA-LEFFLER

illustrated by KRISTINE A. LOMBARDI

Christy Ottaviano Books

Henry Holt and Company • New York

Life was fine and dandy in
the big oak tree on Forest Lane.
Squirrels lived UP,
squirrels lived DOWN,

and in the MIDDLE lived the Gray squirrel family—
Pa, Ma, and Little Zeke.

Everyone played together,

worked together,

and ate together.

The neighborhood was just
the way it should be.

COO COO CAW

Until . . .
SUMMER arrived, and so did a family of birds.
"There goes the neighborhood!" said Pa.
"Those blue jays are bossy and noisy!"

"And their shrieking songs are driving me crazy!" said Ma.

"But I like their singing," said Zeke.

Pa and Ma stuffed the walls with moss
and oak leaves to block out the noise.
"Blue jays don't belong here!"

Pitter-Patter
Chitter-Chatter

Soon AUTUMN arrived, and so did a family of chipmunks.

"There goes the neighborhood!" said Pa. "Chipmunks steal acorns!"

"And they have lots of crying babies!" said Ma.

"But I love babies," said Zeke.

Pa and Ma spent all day hoarding a winter's worth of acorns. They hid them high up in the attic.

"Chipmunks don't belong here."

WINTER arrived.

The birds flew south, and the chipmunks burrowed underground.

The neighborhood was, once again, just the way it should be.

DO NOT DISTURB!

STAY OUT

Until . . .
SPRING arrived, and so did the blue jays,
the chipmunks, and a family of—

SPLIT-CRACK-SPLASH

"BEAVERS!" cheered Zeke.

"Don't be so excited. Beavers are the worst neighbors of all!" said Pa.

"They'll gnaw and chew and destroy everything," said Ma. "Even oak trees!"

"But they build amazing structures!" said Zeke.

"Birds, chipmunks, now beavers? I don't think we belong here," said Pa.

That night, Pa, Ma, and Zeke packed up everything they owned and moved to an old maple tree on the other side of the river.

The Gray family settled into their new home.
"Look, Zeke! There are lots of squirrels here,
just like you," said Ma. "Go up and play!"

Instead, Zeke looked across the river.
He heard the blue jays singing,
the baby chipmunks crying,
and the beavers building.
Zeke missed his friends.

That night, Zeke decided to go and visit
the oak tree.
Slowly he made his way, carefully balancing
on the branches as he crossed the river below.

Suddenly the sky got dark.
Down came the rain,
    down came the hail . . .

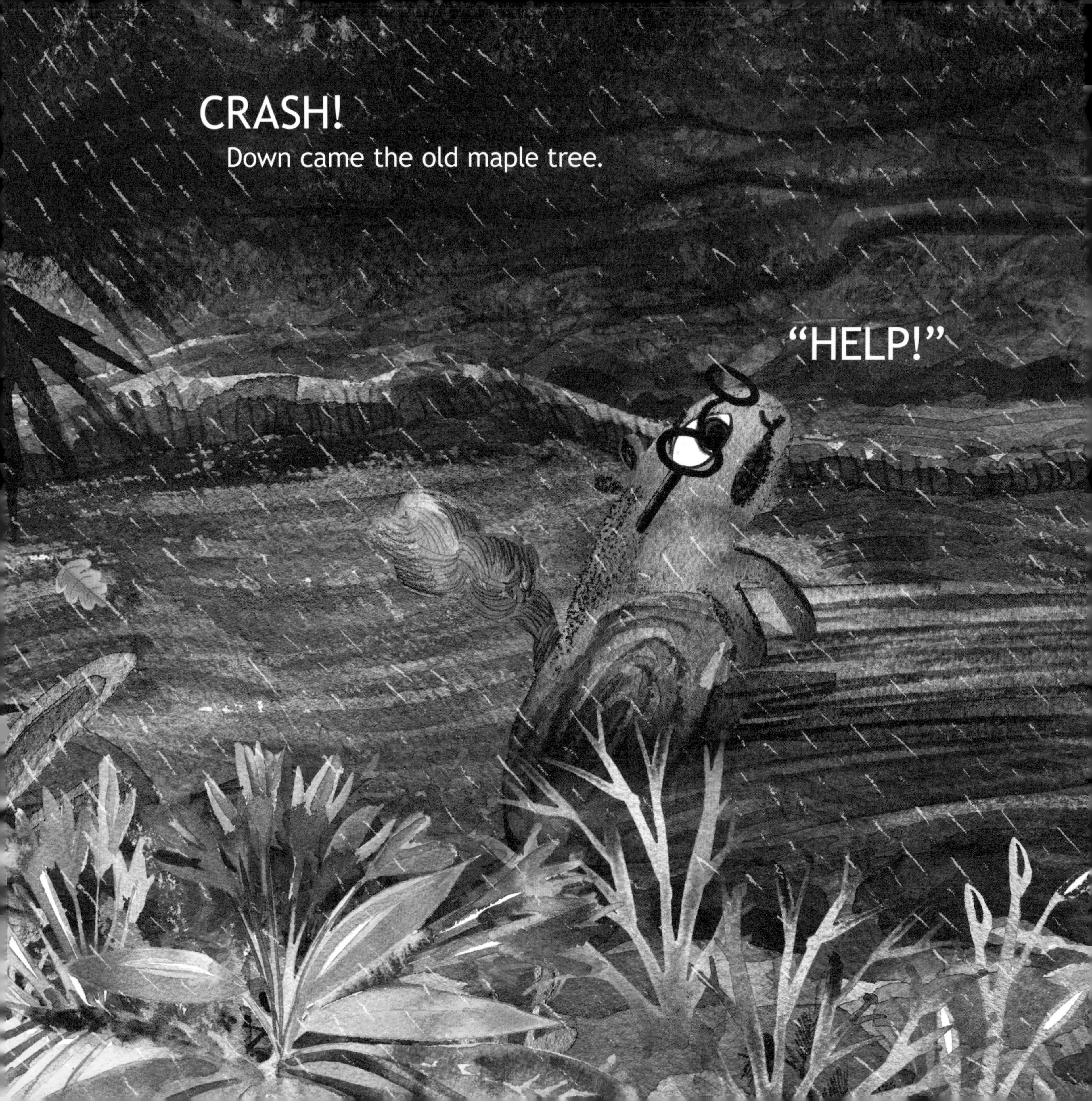

CRASH!

Down came the old maple tree.

"HELP!"

Just then, two blue jays appeared. They lifted Zeke into the sky and carried him to safety.

Downriver, the beavers quickly got to work building a dam, rescuing Ma and Pa.

WELCOME

Back at the oak tree, the chipmunks met them with dry leaves and warm acorn soup.

Life is now fine and dandy in the big oak tree on Forest Lane.
   Blue jays live UP.
      Chipmunks and beavers live DOWN.
      And in the MIDDLE lives the Gray squirrel family—
Pa, Ma, and Little Zeke.

Everyone plays together,
    works together,
        and eats together.
And the neighborhood is just the way it should be.